Fog Island

I dedicate this book to Ireland
and to all the wonderful people
who welcomed us here.

Tomi Ungerer

Fog Island

Φ

Finn and Cara were brother and sister.
They lived by the sea in the back of beyond.

While their father was out fishing,
their mother ran the farm.
They grew and raised what they needed.
The family was poor yet grateful
to survive on what they had.

Finn and Cara looked after the sheep
that grazed the headland.

They loaded the peat, cut and dried
for the hearth.

In the evenings, inside their cottage,
the louder the howling and rattling wind,
the cozier they felt.

Their father was also a boat builder.
From bent reeds and tarred canvas
he fashioned a small *curragh*
as a surprise for the children.

"Never leave the bay," he warned them,
"and stay clear of Fog Island!
It's a doomed and evil place,
surrounded by treacherous currents.
Those who have ventured there
have never returned."

And there in the distance,
miles offshore, Fog Island loomed
like a jagged black tooth.

Finn and Cara loved to explore the
shoreline, and fish on their own.
But one day, a thick fog rolled in
and the tide pulled them out.
Swept up by strong currents, they
drifted out to sea.
They were lost in total silence
but for the warning bell of the buoy.

Darkness slowly fell and the current
carried them to a small inlet.
They dragged their boat ashore and
prepared themselves to spend the night.
As the moon rose and flooded the shore
with a milky light, a stairway carved
into the cliff became visible.

Looking around, Finn exclaimed:
"This must be Fog Island.
Let's find out where those steps lead."

The steps were steep and slippery
and in the moonlight, everything
seemed to be dusted with flour.
They climbed and climbed and climbed…

At last they reached a door set into
a high stone wall.
They rang the bell and the door opened
slowly, squeaking on its rusty hinges.
There stood a wizened old man.

"What a surprise!" he exclaimed. "What brings
you here? Who are you? Anyway, whoever
you are, come inside and be welcome."

They entered a large cavernous hall, curiously warm and steamy.

"I am the Fog Man," said their host.

"You must have got lost in my fog."

"What do you mean, *your* fog?" asked Finn.

"I am the one who makes it. I turned it on and now I will turn it off so it will be clear tomorrow for your journey home."

"How do you make the fog?" asked Cara.
"Let me show you," replied the Fog Man,
opening the thick metal door of
an enormous boiler.
"Look down there, what do you see?"

Finn and Cara bent over the hatch

and gazed down into a deep, deep well.

From the bottom, a blazing heat rose

from a glowing, bubbling, liquid red mass.

"It looks like hell!" said Finn.

"No, it's magma – you're looking into

the centre of the earth."

"Like into the crater of a volcano?" asked Cara.

"Exactly," answered the Fog Man.

"You see, when I open the valve, sea water

flows down, evaporates and becomes fog."

"I've been alone here for such a long time.
But to be lonesome is not a reason to get bored.
The animals seem to love my songs, which
I drone on for hours in forgotten languages.
Now, let me entertain you!"

And what a sing-song they all had.
Finn and Cara had never had so much fun.

"You must be starving by now," remarked the
Fog Man. "Here, try some of my stew. My crows
provide me with seaweed and shellfish, which is
my daily fare." It tasted awful but felt strangely
heartening.

After the meal, the Fog Man showed them
to their room for the night.
There they settled down to sleep in the
huge bed, exhausted by their adventures.

The next morning they woke up in the
midst of ruins.
Had it all been a dream? Was the Fog Man a
ghost or an illusion? But then again, the quilt
and the two steaming bowls of stew waiting for
them — where had they come from?

By now they were in a hurry to leave the island
and get home and had no time for questions
without answers.

As predicted, the fog had lifted,
so Finn and Cara set off in their *curragh*.
The currents, which had now reversed,
towed them towards the mainland.

The Fog Man could control the fog
but not the elements.
A strong wind came up and all at once they
found themselves caught in a storm and tossed
about by furious waves.
Frantically, Cara bailed water from the boat
while Finn tried to keep them on course.

At home, their parents had spent a sleepless night fearing the worst. That morning, their father set out with the other fishermen to search for the children. Just in time, they spotted Finn and Cara. After several attempts, they barely managed to hoist them on board their larger *curragh*.

Finn and Cara's mother spotted the boat in the distance. "Are my children aboard?" she cried, running into the water.

They had battled the elements, but had all made it back to the mainland safe and sound. The onlookers were entangled in gossip.

That night all the neighbours gathered at the local pub to celebrate the children's homecoming. Though nobody had ever before returned from Fog Island, not one of the villagers believed their story about the Fog Man. "We can prove it, the bowls and quilt are still there," Finn and Cara said.

But no one had the courage to go back and check.

Weeks later, brother and sister were having supper. Cara found a hair in her soup, and pulled and pulled.

"The Fog Man's," she whispered to Finn. Their parents never found out the reason for their chuckling giggles.

Phaidon Press Limited
Regent's Wharf
All Saints Street
London, N1 9PA

Phaidon Press Inc.
180 Varick Street
New York, NY 10014

www.phaidon.com

This edition © 2013 Phaidon Press Limited
First published in German as *Der Nebelmann*
© 2012 Diogenes Verlag AG Zürich

ISBN 978 0 7148 6535 5
003-0113

A CIP catalogue record for this book
is available from the British Library.

Printed in China